Book Club Edition

WALT DISNEY'S
BAMBI and the BIG SNOW

D E F G   4

GROLIER
BOOK CLUB EDITION

Bambi and his mother lived in the big woods.

They had lived there all through the warm summer and cool autumn.

Now the days were chilly and the nights were cold.

Winter was coming.

One night, while Bambi slept, it snowed.

PLOP! Bambi woke up.
Something cold had landed on his head.
Bambi opened his eyes and looked around.

What was this?
Tiny bits
of white
were floating
in the air.

Bambi walked out into the big woods.
He had never seen anything like this.
Every branch and twig of the big trees
was coated with white.

Bambi stepped carefully onto the white.
It was cold but soft.
He caught some of the floating white bits
in his mouth.
They had no taste.

THUMP! THUMP! Bambi turned.
There was his friend Thumper the rabbit.
"What is this white stuff?" asked Bambi.

"It's called snow,"
said Thumper. "It
falls in winter."

"Snow is fun," said
Thumper. "Come with
me. I'll show you."
So Bambi followed
Thumper through
the white woods.

Soon the two friends came to a cozy nest.
Flower the skunk was asleep inside it.
"Wake up, Flower!" said Thumper.
"Winter has come! The first snow is here!
It's wonderful!"

"Ooh!" Flower yawned.
"What a time to wake me!
Right in the middle of
my winter sleep!"

"Oh, come on, Flower," said Bambi.
"We'll have lots of fun in the snow."
"Well, maybe," said Flower. "I'm not sure."
But he went along with Bambi and Thumper.

Bambi pranced through the snowy woods
on his long legs.

Thumper hopped cheerfully behind him.

But poor Flower had to plow his way
through the deep snow.

"I don't like this one bit," he said.

The three friends came
to the top of a hill.
They looked down on
a pond covered with ice.

DANGER
THIN ICE

A sign warned of danger.
But the animals could not read it.

"Wow, look at that ice!" said Thumper.
"We can slide down the hill right onto it."

"What is ice?" asked Bambi.

"I don't know," said Flower. "But it
doesn't look safe to me."

"Nonsense," said
Thumper. "Watch me.
Here I go! Whee!"

Down the hill went Thumper.
"Sliding looks like fun," said Bambi.
"It looks pretty risky to me," said Flower.
"I'm going to try it," said Bambi.

"This IS fun!" said Bambi as he slid
down the hill.

"Oh, I can't look," said Flower as
he followed. "It's too scary!"

Swoosh! Thumper, Bambi, and Flower
slid onto the ice.

"Isn't this great?" laughed Thumper.

Bambi and Flower did not answer.

Flower was scared.

And Bambi could not stand up on
the slippery ice.

His feet went in all directions!

Thumper laughed and
laughed.
He thought Bambi
looked funny.

Flower kept his balance with the help
of his fluffy tail.

But he was worried.
He did not like
the ice.
"Be careful,
Bambi," said
Flower.

Slowly Bambi stood up on his feet.
"There's nothing to worry about," said
Thumper. "Playing on the ice is fun!"

"Watch me!"
said Thumper.
And he slid
over the ice.

"There's nothing
to it," he said.

"Come on, Bambi,
you try sliding now.
I'll help you,"
said Thumper.

"I don't think I can do it," said Bambi.
"Sure you can," said Thumper.
And he gave Bambi a great big push.

Swoosh! Away went Bambi...right to the middle of the pond.

The ice was thin there, but nobody knew that.

CRA-A-ACK! SNAP!

The ice broke under Bambi!

Down went Bambi into the ice-cold water.

"Help!" cried Bambi.

He tried to get out of the water.

But he could not.

"Uh-oh!" said Flower. "We must do something!"

Suddenly they heard a new noise.

"What's that?" said Flower.

"Watch out—humans!" said Thumper.

Two skiers were coming over the snowy hill.

The skiers saw Bambi in the icy pond.

"Look! There's a fawn in the pond," said one of them. "We must help it."

"Let's get out of here," said Thumper.

So he and Flower ran and hid.

Bambi shivered with fear and cold.

Thumper and Flower watched from their hiding place.

The humans went to the edge of the pond.

They took off their skis.

The man tied a rope around his waist.

The man laid the four skis
side by side on the ice.
He made a sled.
Then he lay down on the sled
and slowly pulled himself forward.

At last the man reached Bambi.

He carefully pulled Bambi out
of the icy water.

Bambi was too cold to be frightened.

Then the woman began to pull them
back to the edge of the pond.

When the man reached the edge of
the pond, he gently picked up Bambi.
The little fawn was hardly breathing.
His eyes were closed.

Bambi lay very still.

"Poor baby!" said the woman.

She dried Bambi off with
her soft woolen scarf.

"There, there," she said.
"You'll soon be all right."

Thumper and Flower looked on from their hiding place.

"What shall we do?" asked Flower.

"We must tell Bambi's mother," said Thumper.

And so off they ran.

Thumper and Flower found Bambi's mother
at home.

"Where is Bambi?" she said as soon as she
saw them. "Is something wrong?"

"He'll be all right," said Thumper. "I think.
But you'd better come."

"He's down at the pond," said Flower.

Bambi's mother led the way.
Thumper and Flower followed.
They raced through the big woods.

Some birds heard the news and flew along.
"Bambi is in danger," they called.
Everyone wanted to help.

At last they got to the hilltop above the pond.

The animals looked down at Bambi.

Bambi's mother could hardly believe what she saw.

Bambi was with two humans!
But they were not hurting him.
They were patting him.
He looked warm and dry.

Soon Bambi stood up
on his shaky legs.
He saw his mother
and his friends.

Bambi ran up the hill to his mother.
Now he was truly safe.

"Promise me, Bambi," said his mother,
"that you will never go on the ice without
asking me first."

"I promise," said Bambi.

The two humans skied away over the hills.
But none of the animals noticed.
They were too busy with Bambi.